A project created by NubeOcho.
In Europe it was done in collaboration with Amnesty
International Spain and Amnesty International Italy.

It is translated into English and Italian, and will be distributed
in the US, Canada, Mexico, Chile, Italy and Spain.

A portion of the proceeds from the sale of this book is
dedicated to protecting human rights worldwide.

é

É G A L I T è

No Water No Bread
Egalité Series

© Text: Luis Amavisca, 2016
© Illustrations: Guridi, 2016
© Edition: NubeOcho, 2017
www.nubeocho.com - info@nubeocho.com

Original title: *Sin agua y sin pan*
Translator: Ben Dawlatly
Text editing: Kim Griffin and Rebecca Packard

Distributed in the United States by
Consortium Book Sales & Distribution

First edition: 2017
ISBN: 978-84-945971-3-8

Printed in China by Asia Pacific Offset,
respecting international labor standards.

FSC
www.fsc.org
MIX
Paper from
responsible sources
FSC® C012521

NO WATER NO BREAD

LUIS AMAVISCA
GURIDI

nubeOCHO

This is the barbed wire fence.

This is one side of the barbed wire fence.

And this is the other side
of the barbed wire fence.

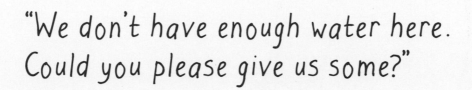

"We don't have enough water here.
Could you please give us some?"

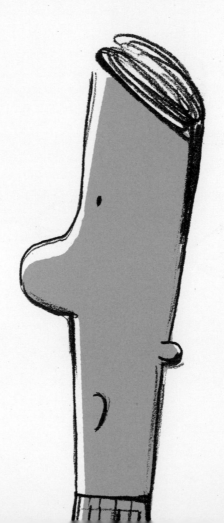

"I'm sorry, it's not on your land.
This is our water."

"We've run out of bread.
Could you please give us a little bit?"

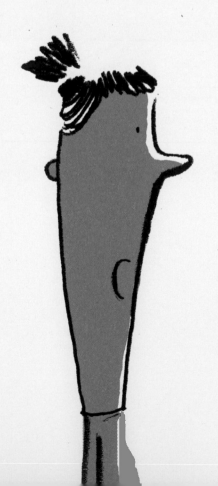

"I'm sorry. This is our bread."

No bread.

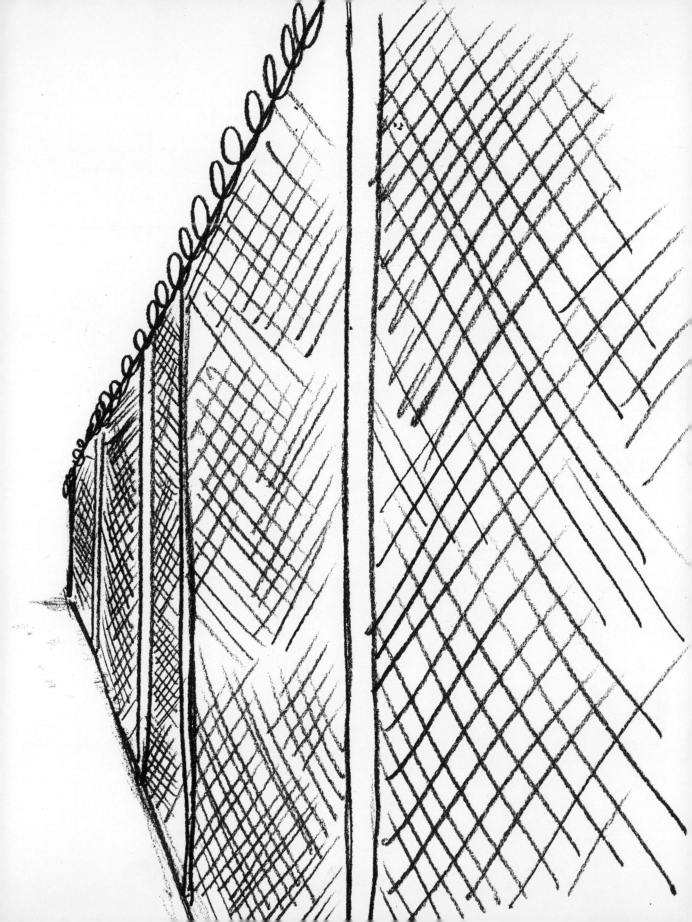

"Could you please give me some bread?"

"Could you please give me some water?"

"Why are our parents like this?"

"Life would be much better…

...without the barbed wire fence."

One day, some strangers came from
a distant land. They had nothing.

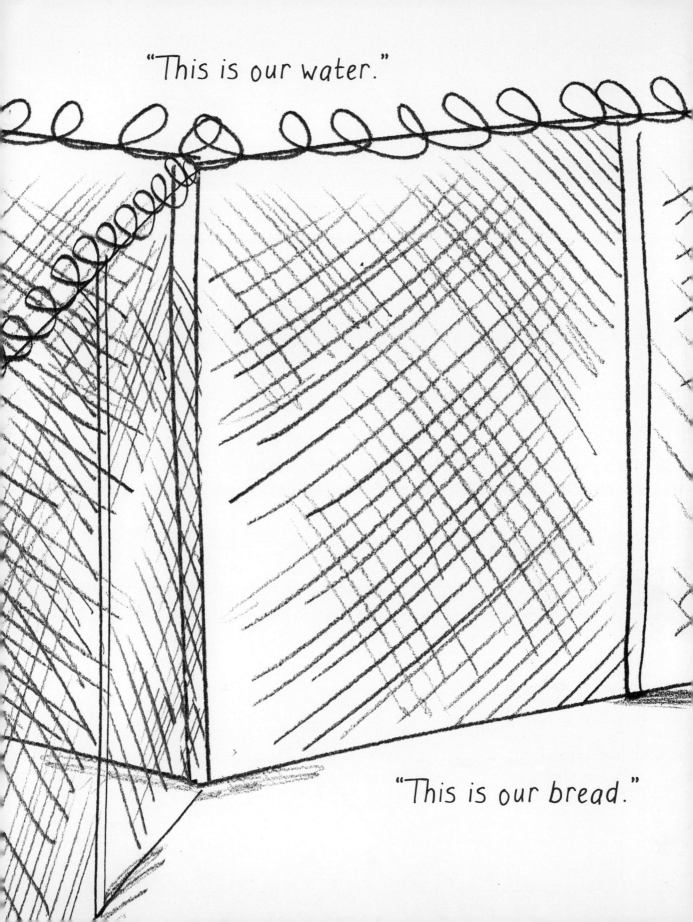